T4-AKT-636

V-two

## THE HERO DISCOVERED

### BY MATT WAGNER

# Mage
V-two [T.M.]

## THE HERO DISCOVERED

Written and Illustrated
by Matt Wagner

Lettered by
Bob Pinaha

Edited by Kay Reynolds,
Gerry Giovinco and
Diana Schutz

## STARBLAZE GRAPHICS

THE DONNING COMPANY/PUBLISHERS
NORFOLK/VIRGINIA BEACH • 1987

**Mage—The Hero Discovered, Volume Two** by Matt Wagner
is one of many graphic novels published by The Donning
Company/Publishers. For a complete listing of our titles, please
write to the address below.

Copyright © 1987 Matt Wagner

All rights reserved, including the right to reproduce this book
in any form whatsoever without permission in writing from
the publisher, except for brief passages in connection with a
review. For information, write:

**The Donning Company/Publishers**
**5659 Virginia Beach Boulevard**
**Norfolk, Virginia 23502**

MAGE was originally published in comic book format by
Comico The Comic Company.

First printing March 1987

10  9  8  7  6  5  4  3  2  1

**Library of Congress Cataloging-in-Publication Data**

Wagner, Matt.
  Mage.
    1. Arthurian romances.   II. Title.
PN6727.W25M3   1987   741.5'973   86-4487
ISBN 0-89865-465-1 (pbk. v. 1)
ISBN 0-89865-467-X (lim. ed.)

**Printed in the United States of America**

# intro

The concept of discovery is a curious one. An Italian mariner, in an effort to establish a trade route to the East, sets sail in the wrong direction, accidentally bumps into a continent, and is forever billed by history as the discoverer of America! A French explorer plants a wooden cross on a mountain-top and thereby "discovers" the city of Montreal—as if, somehow, the land *weren't* there to be found in the first place! Kevin Matchstick nearly trips over an apparent bum in some Philadelphia alleyway and . . . well, wait a minute.

Human beings are kinda curious, too. We often create what we discover—at least in the psychological sense—and then discover what we create. Even more perplexing, we're repeatedly *surprised* by these inner discoveries, as if we had no hand in their making. So it is with Kevin Matchstick.

So it is, too, with friendship. Just as the following chapters of Matchstick's story were beginning to take shape and just as Kevin himself was beginning to find the hero within, I began to discover what would become an abiding friendship with artist Matt Wagner. Oh, I didn't think I would like him much, at first. Our initial contact was over the phone, the summer of '84, from a distance of 3000 miles. I was to interview Matt regarding his plans for this exact segment, strangely enough, of the first part of the **Mage** trilogy. Time and date were set. I made the call—and got his answering machine. Just another flake, I thought. As it turned out, nothing could have been further from the truth.

Skip a beat and spring 1985 found me working with Matt Wagner on a day-to-day basis, editing these very chapters of the **Mage** story line—again, a peculiar synchronicity. Well past my snap judgment of the previous summer, I was to quickly learn that there are precious few people as sincere, as dedicated, and as downright determined as Matt.

The editor/creator relationship can travel a variety of paths, not all of them smooth. The creator, if true to his ideals and to his art (or are these the same?), must constantly strive for an authentic perfection, however one cares to define *that.* The editor, bottom line, must see to it that the work is completed on time. As well as possible, of course, but-baby-make-that-deadline! Naturally, these two rather disparate perspectives lend themselves to a certain potential conflict. It is to Mat Wagner's credit as an artist and a human being that he was able to keep both goals in sight, while never allowing the one to interfere with the other nor compromising himself or Comico, who originally published the following chapters as individual comic books, in any way. Oh, there were a few times, in the course of this run, when Matt did force a modicum of editorial scrambling, but these were balanced by the days on which he would appear at my office door, looking haggard and pasty-faced, clearly not having slept for the three nights previous, but with book in hand and a glimmer of triumph in his spent smile: "It's *done, Di.*"

Matt Wagner is not Kevin Matchstick (though I wouldn't swear to the reverse), but the parallels are obvious. Matt did indeed model his character upon himself and Kevin's physical appearance has changed with his creator's—never mind that Kevin's weight loss occurs, seemingly suddenly, between issues! Some of the parallels are more consciously constructed than others. Chapter eight's "Against a Sea of Troubles" finds Kevin constrained to leave his apartment for good, as the building burns to the ground behind him— the same building, *not* coincidentally, on Philadelphia's Broad Street that housed Matt's studio until, as he was working on that particular chapter, he moved to his current location. Some of the parallels, I dare say, are even unconscious. It is in this portion of the series that Matt, er, Kevin comes to take some of his greatest risks, that he truly discovers (creates) his personal heroism. It is here that he jumps three stories without batting an eyelash, here that he sets a trap for his enemies, here that he moves to confront them. But it is this portion of the series, too, wherein the artist truly takes hold. It is here that Matt Wagner discovers (creates) the definitive look of **Mage I,** here that his facility with color and an airbrush becomes apparent, here that his talent surfaces unrestrained yet highly polished. It is here that the process of discovery really takes place— on all counts.

So too for the editor, the friend, and—most important of all—the reader. These pages don't merely tell Kevin Matchstick's story—or even Matt Wagner's. Rather, these pages hold a meaning that is universal for humankind. You have only to look inside to discover it.

**Diana Schutz**
**July 1987**

# The Story So Far . . .

On his way home one night, Kevin Matchstick, a young man who considers himself very alone in the world, stumbles across Mirth, the cryptic and evasive World-Mage. Following this strange and revelational encounter, Kevin is driven to break up what appears to be a common mugging. But this is hardly so, as Kevin soon realizes that the attacker is not even human, and that he himself is performing feats that are more than human. Still and all, the mugger escapes and the victim dies in Kevin's arms, but not before managing to croak out the strange word "Grackleflint." Kevin reports the death anonymously and returns home in a turmoil, unaware that these recent events have already been noted by a mysterious personage sequestered high in the top of the Styx Hotel Casino.

Arriving home, Kevin is less than surprised to find Mirth already waiting in his living room. When questioned, he explains to Kevin that Emil Grackleflint is the name of the creature that Kevin drove off earlier, and that he is an agent of great evil. Further, he says it is Kevin's destiny to halt this evil. He then quickly departs.

Next morning, Kevin is convinced that all that had gone before was a dream and sets off for work. The subway car, though, is mysteriously empty but for three other passengers. Kevin soon comes to the realization that all of them are Grackleflints. In desperation he leaps through the window directly into the path of the oncoming train.

After the train has roared across his prone body, Kevin is startled to realize that only his clothes have felt the effects. With this experience haunting him, he soon makes his way out via the nearest exit, entirely unaware that he has been spotted by a Grackleflint and his good health reported to the Styx. Stopping to call in sick at work, Kevin once again encounters Mirth. When Kevin demands a private question-and-answer session, Mirth promptly teleports them to the top of a nearby sky-scraper, where he soon learns of Kevin's acute acrophobia.

Relocating at a nearby park, Mirth begins to tell Kevin of his destiny as the hero. The power that has awakened in Kevin, claims Mirth, is needed to defeat the foul Umbra Sprite—the vast evil that has spawned all five of the Grackleflints. The man Kevin saw killed in the alley was a patron of the Endless Struggle. He was murdered because one day he might have become involved. Kevin claims to truly believe none of this, but neither does he deny the evidence of his own eyes. He says he is still an active spectator. These revelations are cut short, though, when Mirth is wracked by a painful bout of The Sight and envisions a lovely girl in a shiny red car at the doubtful mercy of a Grackleflint.

Teleporting to the scene, they are just in time for Kevin to pull back the deadly spur of the Grackleflint, but he soon learns that this Grack (Stanis) can fly. Mirth is forced to enter the fray and strikes the creature down, just as Kevin frantically frees himself from its clutches on high. Falling, Stanis calls forth the shade of his father and is saved. Once again, Mirth must strike out and he succeeds in banishing the Umbra Sprite's shade, but at a high cost to his own powers. Kevin has survived the five-story fall just fine, though, and is taken aback when the young girl they have newly saved falls on her knees

before him. Hastening their exit, Mirth pulls her aside and cautions her against such moves, as he says Kevin is not yet ready to accept his true self, and that he must be made aware slowly.

These new companions then retreat to a local stadium, while the girl introduces herself as Edsel and claims that she had felt inexplicably drawn to follow the creature that had attacked her. Mirth acclaims her a part of the Struggle, and to further this effort, enchants her handy baseball bat. He then proceeds to explain that the Umbra Sprite and his ugly brood are in search of a mystical, shape-changing cripple known as the Fisher King. They desire his blood.

Back at the Styx, Emil arrives to find Stanis and Lazlo "the clairvoyant" anxiously waiting as their father tries to reclaim his banished shade. Whole again, the Umbra Sprite appears before them only to retreat again to begin the summonings of the Marhault Ogre. At the stadium, Kevin is still firm in his disbelief but is soon, again, forced to participate as he is ignominiously grabbed from behind and tossed far into the playing field by the immense Marhault. A vicious battle ensues. Edsel bravely joins in but is hurt, giving Kevin the rage he needs to defeat the evil giant. Following the battle, though, Kevin is morose as he realizes the many civilized veneers that must be dropped in order to win a war. In the midst of this, Mirth is again struck by The Sight and is warned of the authorities that are rapidly approaching the scene. Carrying Edsel, Kevin follows Mirth out a side exit straight into the arms of the police.

Three days later, Kevin sits in his jail cell trying his best to make hs rather seedy cellmates believe that there really was a magician accompanying him and the girl he supposedly kidnapped. Apparently, he just disappeared when the police showed up. His cellmates (Rashem and Gregory) refuse to accept Kevin's claims based on the fact that he says the Mage was white. To prove his point, Kevin concedes to allow himself to be punched in the stomach by Rashem. This test of course fails, though, and Kevin slumps to the floor. Back at the Styx, Emil begins to voice his doubts over their father's competence, as he has done nothing for the past three days but search in vain for the missing Mirth. But as Kevin rises painfully from the floor, the cell is flooded with Green as Mirth comes floating back.

Mirth apologizes to Kevin and claims all the offensive drain on his powers, coupled with being surprised into raising his defenses, caused him to pass out into the safety of the Faerie Realms. But now, he says the time has come for Kevin to use his own power to free himself of the restraints that have been placed upon him by the world of men. He refuses to help in any way and, finally, Kevin is forced to rip out the bars of his cell. and, finally, Kevin is forced to rip out the bars of his cell.

Kevin and Mirth then stop off into the lost time of the Faerie Realms to finish cleaning up the evidence of Kevin's arrest. As they make ready to leave, they are shocked to encounter Sean Knight, Kevin's public defender, deep in the lands and times where no mortal is often seen. They soon discover that Sean is dazed and confused as to his surroundings and, alas, all three are unaware that the Umbra Sprite has sent Lazlo to attack them along with a number of Red Caps.

THE HERO DISCOVERED

# MAGE

™

# CHAPTER 6

Alas, Poor Ghost

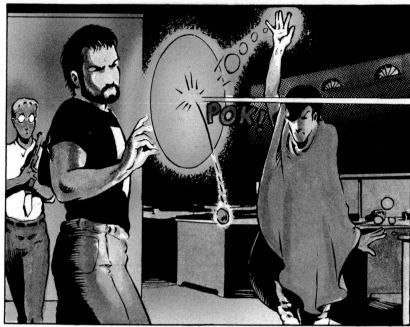

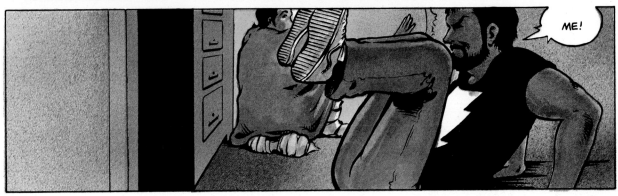

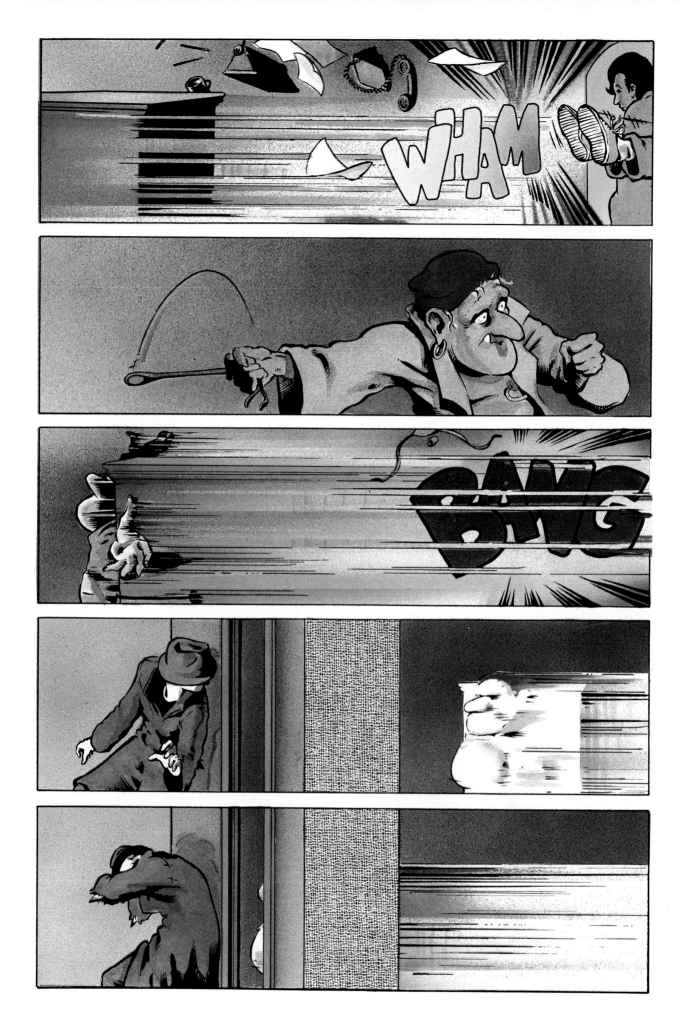

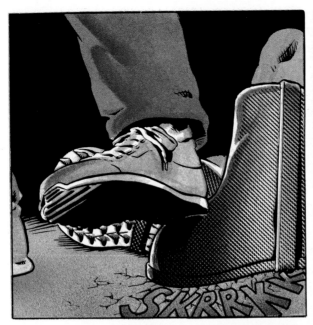

WELL?

HE'S NOT GOIN' ANYWHERE. GO CHECK ON SEAN.

SEAN?

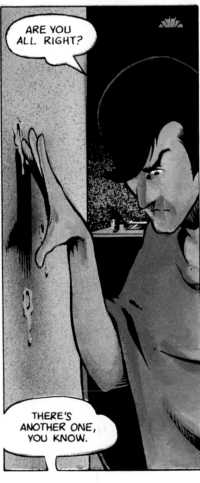

ARE YOU ALL RIGHT?

THERE'S ANOTHER ONE, YOU KNOW.

THE LEADER...

...HE'S GETTING AWAY.

KEVIN...

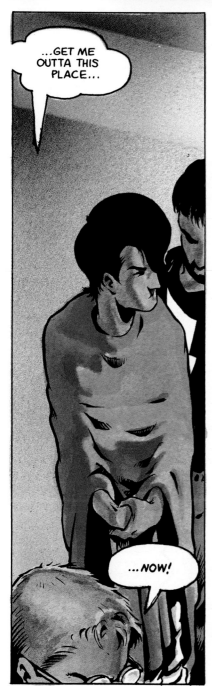

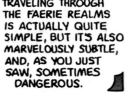

ITS SPITTLE IS DEATH.

THE HAIRY ONE IS BEYOND YOUR GRASP, THOUGH, AND WILL SEEK TO PROTECT THE FOUL MAGICIAN.

LOOK TO STRIKE AT HIM THROUGH THE *JEUNESSE* SLUT YOU WILL SEE JOIN THEM.

DOUBLE LUCKY ARE WE, *RASHEM*.

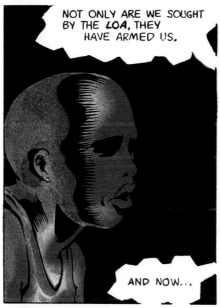

NOT ONLY ARE WE SOUGHT BY THE *LOA*, THEY HAVE ARMED US.

AND NOW...

FZZZ

...LO, THEY GRANT US A COMPANION.

SEEK THEM AT MIDDAY, WHEN THEY CAST NO SHADOW.

LET *BARON SAMEDI* FEAST ON THEIR BONES.

FAREWELL, *RASHEM*, MY LOVE.

WHAT IS IT?

LOOKS LIKE A STAPLE GUN.

WITHOUT MY SHIELDS, THERE SHOULD'VE BEEN NO WAY FOR SEAN TO ESCAPE BEING STRUCK BY AN ELF-BOLT BACK THERE. THERE WERE SEVERAL HOLES IN THE WALL *BEHIND* WHERE HE WAS HUDDLED, YET SEAN WAS UNTOUCHED.

IN FACT THIS *ISN'T* SO UNCOMMON, THOUGH. CONSIDERING HOW RELATIVELY *CONVENIENT* MODERN LIFE HAS BECOME, I'M NOT SURPRISED THIS HAS REMAINED UNDETECTED.

IN FACT...

...I'M SURE THERE ARE ACTUALLY QUITE A FEW GHOSTS OUT THERE LEADING RELATIVELY NORMAL LIVES.

OH BOY.

I DON'T...

I REALLY *DON'T* REMEMBER ANYTHING.

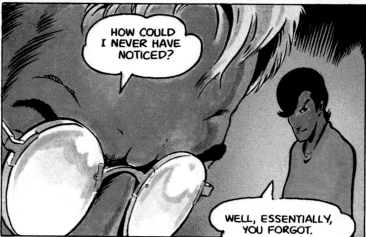

HOW COULD I NEVER HAVE NOTICED?

WELL, ESSENTIALLY, YOU FORGOT.

SO, WHAT NOW?

I'M CONVINCED WE WERE *INTENDED* TO ENCOUNTER YOU, SEAN. IT WOULD SEEM WE NEED EACH OTHER. COME WITH US.

COME WITH YOU? TO JOIN IN SOME FIGHT I KNOW NOTHING ABOUT? OUT THERE...

...WHERE I'M DEAD?

WHY NOT JUST STAY HERE? FROM WHAT YOU SAID, I'LL EVENTUALLY LOSE IT ALL--A MINDLESS SPIRIT TRAPPED BY THE ROUTINE OF ITS LIFE. I MIGHT AS WELL JUST SIT AGAINST THIS WALL AND WAIT.

BUT COULD YOU DO THAT? COULD YOU BEAR TO JUST SIT AND WAIT? YOU DON'T BELONG HERE, *SEAN*, AND YOU DON'T BELONG OUT THERE. YOUR PLACE IS BEYOND AND YET YOU SUFFER UNREST.

YOUR GOAL IS WITH US. TRUST ME, THIS WAS NOT INCIDENTAL.

BUT, WHY SHOULD I TRUST YOU?! WHY?!

GOD, LOOK AT *HIM!* HE'S ONE OF THE PLAYERS AND *HE* DOESN'T BELIEVE! YOU CAN SEE IT IN HIS FACE!

WELL, YOU HAVE TO UNDER- STAND ABOUT KEVIN, HE DOESN'T BELIEVE IN MUCH OF ANYTHING.

DO YOU?    NO, I DON'T.

EASE UP, YOU.

BUT, HOW CAN YOU DO THAT? HOW CAN YOU GO ALONG, WHEN YOU'RE IN SUCH DOUBT?

IF YOU DOUBT EVERY- THING, YOU'RE NEVER DISAPPOINTED.

AND NEVER GRATIFIED, EITHER.

MAN, *THAT'S* MESSY THINKING.

SAY, *MIRTH*, IF I *DON'T* BELIEVE YOU, WILL I END UP LIKE HIM?

COULD BE...

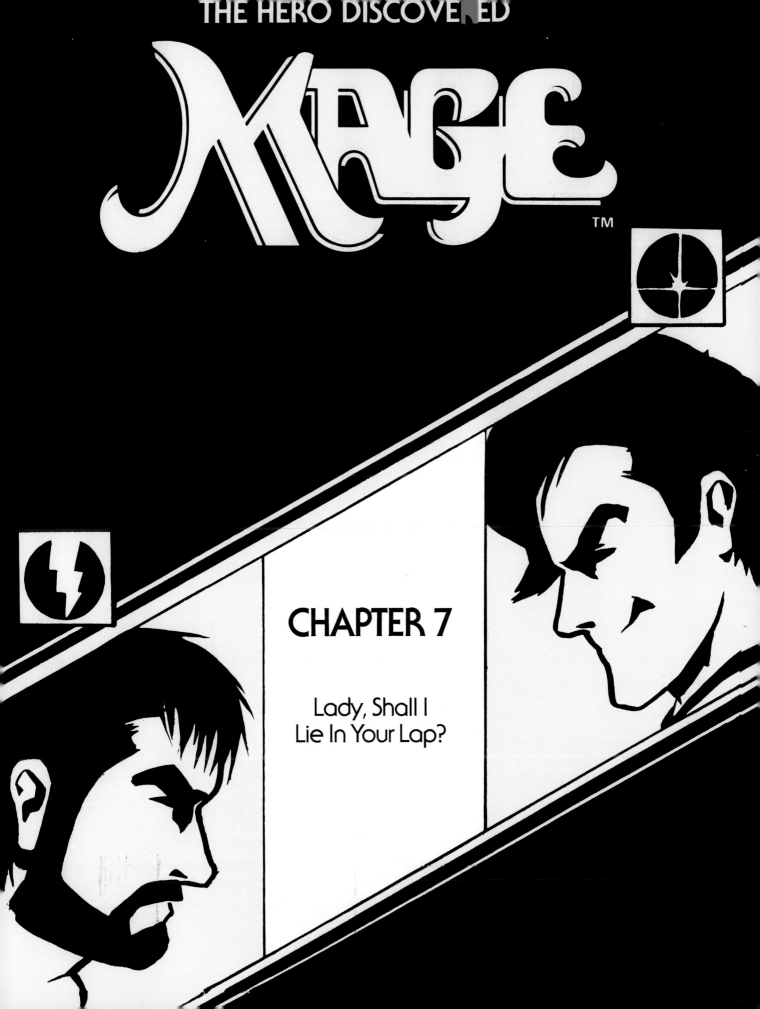

SO, *SEAN*, THE FACT THAT YOU'RE *DEAD* BECOMES AN OBSTACLE ONLY IN YOUR OWN MIND. IT'S SIMPLY A STATE OF EXISTENCE DIFFERENT FROM THE ONE THAT YOU *THOUGHT* YOU WERE EXPERIENCING. AND, OF COURSE, WITH THIS CHANGE COMES A CHANGE IN THE *FACILITIES* YOU'RE USED TO. YOUR FUNCTION HAS CHANGED AND, THEREFORE, SO HAVE YOUR FUNCTIONINGS.

EVERYTHING'S BEFORE YOU. YOU SIMPLY DON'T KNOW WHERE THE ON/OFF SWITCH IS. THAT'S WHY YOU WERE STRUCK WITH A CASE OF *THE SIGHT* BACK THERE--AND HOW YOU SLIPPED INTO THE FAERIE REALMS IN THE FIRST PLACE. IT'S EASILY TRIGGERED, BUT THE *AIMING'S* A BIT TENUOUS.

WAIT A MINUTE...

...Y'MEAN LIKE *POWERS?* I'VE GOT *GHOST* POWERS?

WELL, OF COURSE.

SHIT.

I'M AFRAID I'M NOT GOING TO BE TOO COOPERATIVE, HERE.

BUT I DON'T...

NOW, GIVE ME A BREAK, HERE. FIFTEEN MINUTES AGO, YOU CONVINCED ME I'M DEAD.

AND *NOW* YOU WANT ME TO BREAK OUT THE SHEETS AND CHAINS.

I *JUST* DON'T THINK I CAN GIVE THAT MUCH. ISN'T IT *ENOUGH* THAT I'VE AGREED TO GO ALONG WITH WHATEVER LITTLE WAR YOU'RE WAGING? I'LL HELP YOU ANY WAY I CAN, BUT MY REALITY'S ALREADY BEEN SCREWED UP ENOUGH TO ADD ALL *THIS* TO IT YET.

I'M SORRY, THIS JUST *ISN'T* "SEAN, THE FRIENDLY GHOST."

AND, SO, YOU'RE JUST AS BAD AS I AM.

HUH?

NOW, TELL ME WHO'S WORSE: *ME*, FOR GOING ALONG WITH SOMETHING I CAN'T BELIEVE, OR *YOU*, WHO WON'T FULLY JOIN IN WHAT YOU'VE *ALREADY* ACCEPTED.

THE DEFENSE RESTS.

*VERY* WELL, MIRTH...

...TEACH ME HOW TO BE A GHOST.

SO, AS I WAS SAYING...

...ALL OF THESE NEW ...*FACILITIES* STEM FROM THE FACT OF YOUR NEW CONDITION. SINCE YOU'RE NO LONGER ALIVE, YOU NOW OPERATE ON AND ARE SUBJECT TO AN *ENTIRELY DIFFERENT* SYSTEM OF ENERGY. IT'S THE SOURCE OF YOUR POWER, *AND* OF YOUR GROWING AMNESIA. YOUR MIND NO LONGER USES THE NORMAL ELECTROMAGNETIC IMPULSES IT'S BEEN USED TO, SO ALL YOUR STORED MEMORIES ARE GRADUALLY SLIPPING AWAY. BUT, *BECAUSE* OF THIS, YOU HAVE A CERTAIN AMOUNT OF CONTROL OVER ELECTRICAL IMPULSES. YOU'RE SOMEWHAT OF AN EMPTY BATTERY.

EARLIER, I SAID THAT YOUR PLACE WAS NEITHER HERE NOR THERE, BUT SOMEWHERE BEYOND. UNTIL YOU REACH THAT GOAL, YOU ARE FREE TO TRAVEL AMONG THE OTHER LAYERS AT WILL.

IN SHORT, YOU'RE *INTANGIBLE*... IF YOU SO DESIRE.

NOW, COME ON, GIVE IT A TRY. THE TRICK IS TO REACH. AFTER ALL, YOU'RE NOT WHERE YOU WANT TO BE.

ARE YOU?

...DOES THIS GET EASIER? OR IS IT THE *VERY DIFFICULTY* THAT FIRES YOUR DISBELIEF?

*SEE? NOTHING TO IT.*

NOW, TAKE IT OUT.

YES... WELL, YOUR CONTROL CAN ONLY IMPROVE.

BELIEVE ME...

TELL ME, KEVIN...

I'VE GOT *NO HOPE* OF CONTROL, COUNSELOR. MY NEW "*FACILITIES*" OCCUR WHETHER *I* LIKE IT OR NOT. *THEY* DECIDE WHEN AND WHERE.

WHEN THIS ALL STARTED, I GOT RUN OVER BY A SUBWAY TRAIN AND THAT WAS WEIRD. RIGHT BACK THERE, I JUMPED THROUGH AN ELEVATOR CAR AND *THAT* WAS EMBARRASSING.

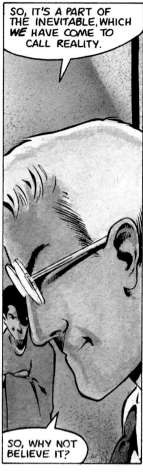

SO, IT DOESN'T MATTER *HOW* I FEEL ABOUT IT OR HOW *USED* TO IT I GET, IT *STILL* HAPPENS.

SO, IT'S A PART OF THE INEVITABLE, WHICH *WE* HAVE COME TO CALL REALITY.

SO, WHY NOT BELIEVE IT?

WELL, IT DOESN'T ASK FOR MY APPROVAL, DOES IT?

I DON'T AFFORD IT MINE.

DOES HE *BELIEVE* THAT?

I'M AFRAID SO.

ISN'T IT, THOUGH?

ANYWAY, AS TO WHOM WE'RE UP AGAINST IN THIS WHOLE THING...

THAT'S JUST AMAZING.

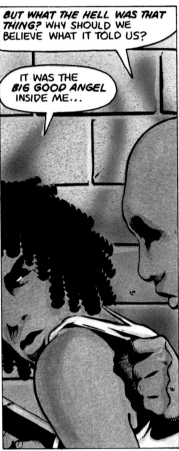

I WOKE UP IN THE BACK OF AN *AMBULANCE* WITH *COPS* ALL OVER THE PLACE AND MY POP JUST *A'FUMIN'* MAD, AND I'VE BEEN GROUNDED EVER SINCE. I TAKE IT HE *BEAT* THAT THING.

SURE DID.

THANKS, DRAPES.

SO, HOW'D YOU GET NAILED?

WE DALLIED A LITTLE TOO LONG, BUT *I* WASN'T APPREHENDED. ONLY KEVIN.

YEAH, SO I FIGURED. DAD RANTS AND RAVES ABOUT WHO *"THE BIG HAIRY WHITE GUY"* IS, BUT HE NEVER MENTIONED A THING ABOUT YOU. THANKS FOR GRABBIN' THE BAT.

YOU'RE WELCOME.

SO, HOW WAS THE STAY, KEV?

ENLIGHTENING.

I'LL BET.

WHO'S HE?

OH, SO SORRY, MY DEAR. THIS IS *SEAN*, THE LATEST ADDITION TO OUR LITTLE CIRCLE. HE'S A GHOST.

HI.

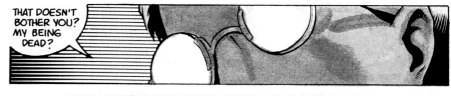

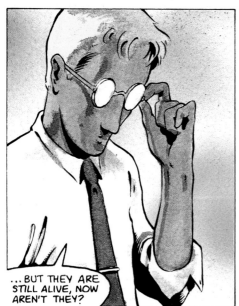

NOPE, JUST TAKES MY KEYS AND PARKS M'CAR IN THE ALLEY.

YEAH, WE SAW. THAT'S ENOUGH?

DAMN STRAIGHT. WITHOUT MY CAR, I DON'T WANNA GO NOWHERE.

BESIDES, I'VE GOT HER FIXED UP SPECIAL. SHE DOESN'T START WITHOUT THE KEYS.

≡AHEM≡

YOU'RE A GEM, DRAPES.

SO, FILL ME IN. WHERE TO NEXT?

KEVIN'S APARTMENT. WE'VE GOT TO TAKE ADVANTAGE OF THESE APPARENTLY PEACEFUL MOMENTS AND START GETTING ORGANIZED.

LIKE I SAID, I GOT 'ER RIGGED UP HERE AND THERE. BESIDES, I KNEW HOW TO HANDLE THE OL' BAT LONG BEFORE DRAPES MADE IT A "LIGHT-STICK!"

HEY, EDSEL, AREN'T YOU WORRIED ABOUT YOUR DAD PARKING YOUR CAR IN THIS ALLEY? THIS THING'S PRETTY OLD.

SPEAKIN' O' WHICH, AIN'T THERE ANY WAY TO TURN THIS THING OFF, ONCE IN A WHILE?

I'M AFRAID NOT, MY DEAR--ONE OF THE DRAWBACKS OF THAT SPELL.

BUT IT MIGHT CONCEIVABLY GIVE US AWAY SOMETIME.

BUT IT MIGHT ALSO BLIND AND SMITE OUR ENEMIES.

NOT IF THEY HIT US FIRST.

BUT THEY HAVE HIT, MY FRIEND--AGAIN AND AGAIN. AND THEY'VE YET TO SUCCEED.

SO IF THEY ARE BLIND, THEN NOW WE SHALL SMITE.

WELL, THAT JUST MIGHT NOT BE GOOD ENOUGH. I'VE JUST RECEIVED WORD FROM *PIET*-- WE'VE GOT *ANOTHER* LEAD. THERE'S A NEW FACE DOWN AT THE MISSION ON SOUTH AND THIRD.

AND THERE'S NO CHANCE OF A FAKE THIS TIME--GUY'S ONLY GOT ONE FOOT.

WE NEED LAZLO'S TALENTS.

*FZZ*

SO TAKE *RADU* OFF SEARCH AND PUT HIM ON SURVEILLANCE. COVER THE LITTLE *CRIP* FOR A WHILE.

*SNAP!*

*NINE DAYS?* IF IT *IS* THE *FISHER KING*, THAT'S NEXT TO IMPOSSIBLE.

*UNNNGH--*

WHAT IS IT?

THEY'RE ON THEIR WAY TO *MATCHSTICK'S* APARTMENT.

I *MUST* SEE TO THEIR RECEPTION.

SO, WHAT ABOUT *RADU?*

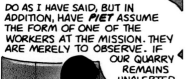

DO AS I HAVE SAID, BUT IN ADDITION, HAVE *PIET* ASSUME THE FORM OF ONE OF THE WORKERS AT THE MISSION. THEY ARE MERELY TO OBSERVE. IF OUR QUARRY REMAINS UNALERTED, THERE SHOULD BE NO REASON FOR HIM TO RUN.

BUT THAT'LL TIE UP *TWO* OF US!

EMIL...

...WHILE I'M BUSY, WHY DON'T YOU GO CHECK ON LAZLO'S WOUNDS?

YES, SIR.

SO, AS SOON AS WE CAN EFFECTIVELY DISGUISE OUR MOVEMENTS, WE START SEARCHING FOR WHERE THE *UMBRA SPRITE* AND HIS BROOD HAVE HOLED UP ON THIS WORLD.

WE HAVE *NO* IDEA WHERE THEY'RE AT?

NONE.

WE'VE BEEN GIVEN A LOT OF EXTRAS, *SPOOK.* WE *CAN'T* HAVE IT ALL.

FAB.

*THAT'S* A FATALISTIC OPTIMISM.

*THAT'S* BULLSHIT.

WELL, HOW HARD CAN THIS BE? I MEAN, THEY *DO* KINDA STAND OUT IN A CROWD.

PROBABLY NOT. THEIR FATHER'S NO SLOUCH, SO WE *CAN'T* BE SURE HOW EVERYBODY ELSE IS SEEING THEM. THEY'RE MOST LIKELY WELL DISGUISED.

SHOULDA SEEN *THAT* COMING.

BUT HOW DO THEY KEEP FINDING US?

YOU *SURE* IT'S NOT THE BAT?

LOOK, IT'S *NOT* THE BAT. BUT IF EVERYONE'S *SO* CONCERNED ABOUT IT...

I'M NOT.

JUST COVERING ALL ANGLES...

...IF EVERYONE *ELSE* IS SO WORRIED, WE'LL MAKE A SLIPCOVER OF SOME SORT FOR IT.

LISTEN, WHY DOESN'T SOMEONE WHIP UP A POT OF COFFEE? I'VE *GOTTA* CHANGE--I'VE BEEN WEARIN' THIS STUFF FOR THE LAST FIVE DAYS. EVERYTHING'S OUT IN THE KITCHEN.

JUST *DYING* TO WALLOW IN WHAT'S UNDER THE MESH.

DON'T YOU *SEE*, TINY BOY, THE HAZARD YOU'RE IN?

BUT I SEE YOU SEE NOT...

IN WHICH CASE, I *WIN*.

WONDER IF KEVIN HAS ANY GAUZE?

ASK HIM.

YOU'RE BRILLIANT SOMETIMES.

AND YOU'RE *ALWAYS* A SMART-ASS.

PART OF THE CHARM.

UH-HUH.

HEY, KE--

SLAM!

UH-OH.

WE'VE GOT A PROBLEM HERE, PEOPLE.

LIKE--?

SOMEONE FOUND US AGAIN. THERE'S A *LEANHAUN SIDHE* IN THERE WITH *KEVIN*.

"LEE-ANNAN SHE"?

A FAERIE MISTRESS. THEY SEDUCE MEN AND DRINK THEIR BLOOD. IF THEY CATCH YOU OFF GUARD, YOU'RE *PRACTICALLY* DEFENSELESS. I'M NOT SURE HOW BADLY SHE'S GOT HIM YET, BUT IT DIDN'T LOOK GOOD.

WELL, CAN'T YOU *DO* SOMETHING?

UNFORTUNATELY, *NO*. I'VE HAD SOME TROUBLES WITH HER KIND IN THE PAST.

I WAS LUCKY SHE DIDN'T SEE ME.

'SCUSE ME, GENTLEMEN.

YOU'RE GOING TO LET HER--

SHE'S THE ONLY ONE WHO *CAN* DO SOMETHING, *SEAN*.

HEY, MAKE SURE YOU CLOSE THAT DOOR, TOO.

UH-HUH.

UHNN-GH...

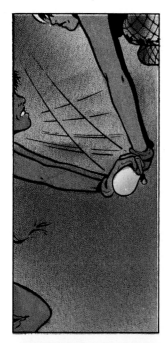

SO, A MISSY JUMPS IN
WITH WEAPON AND SPUNK

TO SAVE HIM
BY WHOM THEY
ARE LED.

SO, WE'LL SEE HOW HE LIKES YOU,
YOU MEDDLESOME PUNK,

WITH YOUR
FACE NOW
ALL MANGLED
AND RED.

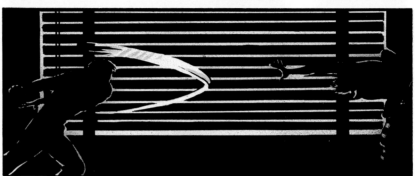

SP∞M!

WELL?

I JUST HEARD A BIG, FUNNY NOISE AND NOW EVERYTHING'S QUIET.

A...AG...G-GRACKLEFLINT...

WHERE?

NOT FOR LONG, I'M AFRAID--

M-M-MIRTH...

K-KANG!

SEAN, JUST *RELAX!* BREATHE DEEPLY... AND TELL ME WHAT YOU SEE.

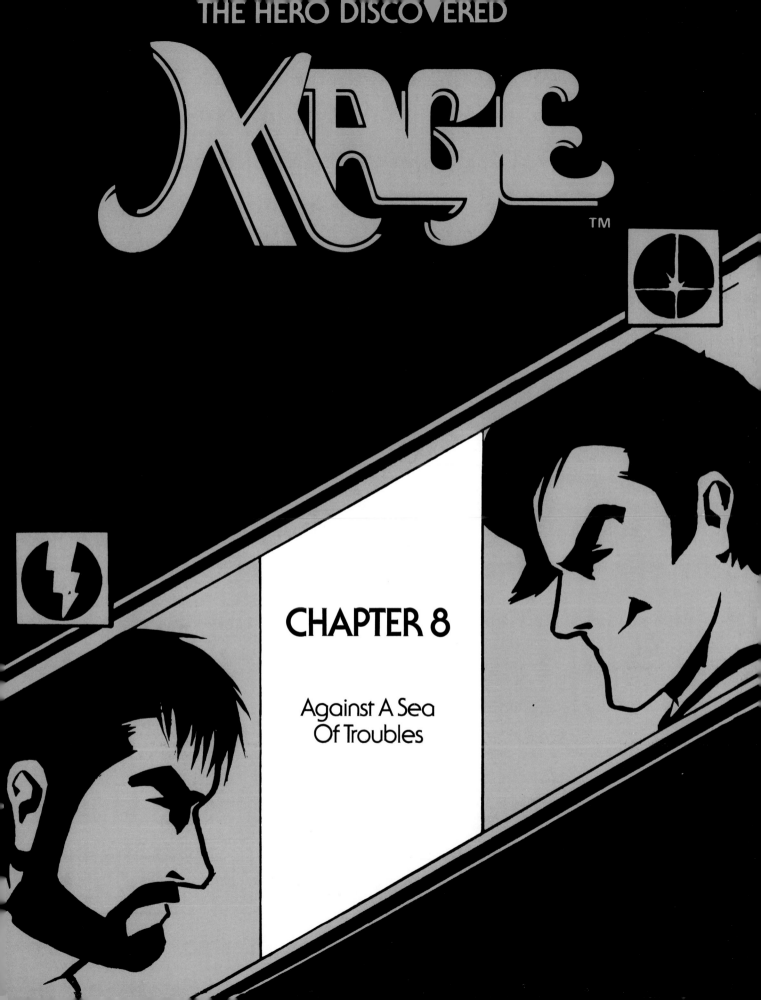

OK, NOW WAIT A MINUTE. FIRST OFF, WHO THE HELL WAS THAT FISHNET NIGHTMARE THAT JUST EXPLODED AGAINST MY WALL?

WELL, I DON'T KNOW HER PARTICULAR NAME, KEVIN, BUT THAT WAS A LEANHAUN SIDHE.

UH-HUH.

A FAERIE MISTRESS. REALLY NASTY.

AND, SO, JUST WHERE WERE YOU?

OH, I'M AFRAID I WOULD'VE BEEN JUST NO HELP AT ALL IN THIS CASE. SEAN EITHER, FOR THAT MATTER.

IN FACT, ANY MALE'S PRETTY SUSCEPTIBLE. WE'RE JUST LUCKY WE STOPPED TO GET EDSEL BEFORE COMING HERE.

BUT, HOW'D SHE GET HERE?

THE UMBRA SPRITE, OF COURSE.

SO, NOW THEY'RE HERE, TOO! NOT JUST OUT THERE! NOW THEY KNOW WHERE I LIVE.

I'M AFRAID HE'S MOST LIKELY KNOWN FOR QUITE SOME TIME.

AFTER ALL, I FOUND YOU WITH NO TROUBLE.

AW, DAMN.

NOT SO GLUM, KEVIN. THIS COULD BE JUST THE CHANCE WE NEEDED.

HOW SO?

YOUR *WHAT?*

MY DE-*LIGHTFUL* PLEASURE. NUTHIN' LIKE A GOOD SCRAP.

'SIDES, *YOU* DIDN'T SEEM TO BE DOIN' ANY TOO SLICK.

UH-HUH.

OKAY, DRAPES, HOW DO WE GET OL' PASTY, THERE, TO CRACK? IN GENERAL, IT JUST DOESN'T LOOK LIKE HE'S GONNA BE A VERY OPEN PERSON.

*THAT'S* PUTTING IT MILDLY.

SO, WHAT DO YA SAY? CAN I USE THE BAT?

NO, OF COURSE NOT.

WE'RE THE *GOOD* GUYS, REMEMBER?

WELL, EVEN THE GOOD GUYS GET MEAN SOMETIMES.

I'LL SAY.

LOOK, I'M PARTICI-PATING. GIMME A BREAK.

YES, YOU'RE GETTING *MUCH* BETTER TOO, SEAN.

BUT I'M AFRAID YOU CAN TURN IT OFF, NOW.

THIS WON'T BE MUCH TROUBLE.

WE WON'T BE NEEDING THE LIGHT, *OR* THE BAT, *OR* THE MUSCLE.

Y'SEE, GRACS CAN'T STAND WATER.

SEAN, COME WITH US, WILL YOU?

NNMPH! NUMPHA-UNGHH!

SEAN? YO, *MIRTH*, WHAT ABOUT ME?

I SUGGEST YOU CLEAN UP THAT SPILLED POT OF COFFEE AND GET STARTED ON A NEW BATCH.

RIGHT IN HERE, STAN.

Y'MEAN *I* DON'T GET TO BE IN ON THE QUESTIONING? HOW COME? AND *WHY* IN THE BATHROOM?

THERE'S A SHOWER IN THE BATHROOM...

MMNPH! NNUD HHMPFF!

...AND, *NO*, I'LL ONLY NEED *SEAN* FOR THE INTERROGATION.

JUST A MOMENT...

BACK IN A FLASH, *STAN*, YOU JUST WAIT HERE... AND *DON'T* KICK AROUND TOO MUCH. MIGHT JUST RINSE YOUR- SELF DOWN THE DRAIN.

YOU SEE, I DON'T *WANT* TO TORTURE THE DAMNED CREATURE, AND IF *SEAN'S* THERE I WON'T HAVE TO.

COME AGAIN?

SEAN'S A GHOST. HE CAN *OOZE* FEAR IF HE WANTS. WE'LL SPOOK THE INFO OUT OF HIM. *I'VE* BEEN BUILDING A SCARE IN HIM, BUT SEAN'S WHAT WE NEED NOW.

STAN'LL SPILL HIS GUTS AND *WE* WON'T SPILL A DROP.

REALLY?

GIVE 'ER A TRY, SEAN. START TO FEEL SCARY--*REAL* GRUESOME.

WHOA!

YES, *THAT'S* IT! NOW, COME WITH ME.

KEVIN, HOW 'BOUT THAT COFFEE?

WHAT D'YA MEAN YOU'RE "IT"?

I'M THE TRAITOR IN OUR MIDST. I'M THE MAGIC "BEACON" THAT'S BEEN LEADING OUR FOES TO US AGAIN AND AGAIN.

HOW?

MAGIC, ITSELF, IS BEST DESCRIBED AS A RIVER. ANY USER OF ITS WATERS MUST DIP INTO ITS SWIFT AND RESTLESS DEPTHS.

ITS COLOR IS THEN PERVERTED, DEPENDING ON ITS USE.

AND, SO, WHAT DOES GREEN INDICATE?

GREEN IS PURE. THE RIVER IS GREEN.

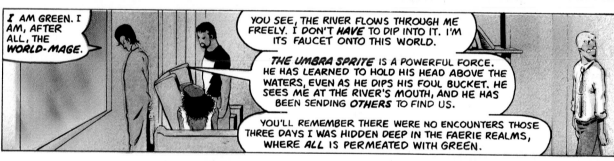

I AM GREEN. I AM, AFTER ALL, THE WORLD-MAGE.

YOU SEE, THE RIVER FLOWS THROUGH ME FREELY. I DON'T HAVE TO DIP INTO IT. I'M ITS FAUCET ONTO THIS WORLD.

THE UMBRA SPRITE IS A POWERFUL FORCE. HE HAS LEARNED TO HOLD HIS HEAD ABOVE THE WATERS, EVEN AS HE DIPS HIS FOUL BUCKET. HE SEES ME AT THE RIVER'S MOUTH, AND HE HAS BEEN SENDING OTHERS TO FIND US.

YOU'LL REMEMBER THERE WERE NO ENCOUNTERS THOSE THREE DAYS I WAS HIDDEN DEEP IN THE FAERIE REALMS, WHERE ALL IS PERMEATED WITH GREEN.

HE--AH-- HE COULDN'T FIND ME, YOU SEE.

SO VERY MUCH TO REMEMBER...

ANYWAY, I'M AFRAID ONCE AGAIN...

...I HAVE TO LEAVE.

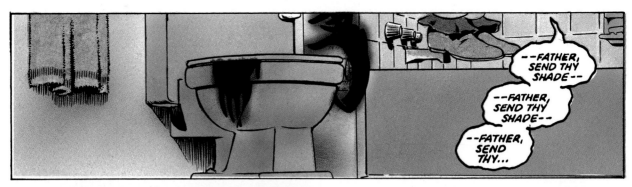

WHAT?

HE'S *LOOSE!*

C'MON!

DOESN'T SMELL. HE DIDN'T "POP" OUT.

NO WINDOWS.

ONE OF THE DRAINS, THEN.

ISN'T HE A LITTLE BIG?

AND I THOUGHT YOU SAID NO WATER.

WELL, HE OBVIOUSLY HAD HELP, BUT THE WATER *WOULD* PRESENT A PROBLEM. HE PROBABLY COULDN'T HAVE TAKEN HIM VERY FAR...

WHERE'S THE NEAREST WINDOW THAT LOOKS ONTO YOUR STREET?

IN THE FRONT HALL.

IF HE COMES UP THROUGH A SEWER-HOLE, MAYBE WE'LL SEE HIM. IF *NOT,* WE TAKE MORE *DRASTIC* STEPS.

JOY.

BINGO, KEV! *THERE* Y'GO!

UH-HUH.

AH, VERY GOOD.

THINK THAT'S *HIS* BUG?

DOUBT IT SERIOUSLY.

BOY, THOSE GUYS ARE OBSTINATE.

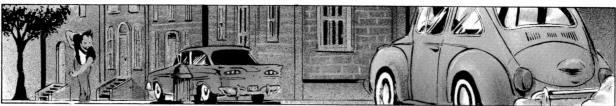

WAAHH--

OUMPFGH!!!

SURREPT-T

O--MI--GOD--

=SIGH=

WOW.

JUST, WOW.

SKRT-T WAP-T WAP

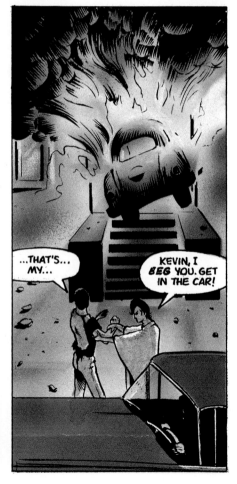

DAMMIT, MIRTH, THAT'S MY BUILDING! MY APARTMENT IS BURNING DOWN! EVERYTHING I HAVE!

KEVIN, YOU KNOW WE CAN'T STAY HERE. I SWEAR TO YOU THAT IF YOU DON'T GET IN THE CAR, I WILL TELEPORT AWAY WITH YOU.

PLEASE, KEVIN, DON'T MAKE ME...

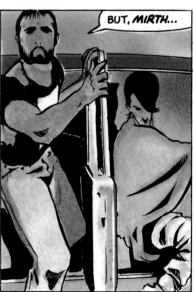

BUT, MIRTH...

...I'M BURNING UP BACK THERE.

IT IS **NOW** EVIDENT TO ME THAT SEAN **WAS** MEANT TO FILL THE GAP THAT **I** WOULD LEAVE-- NOT A MAGE, BUT CERTAINLY UNTRACEABLE. STILL, CAPABLE HANDS WIELD LIMITED POWER IN THE GREATEST OF WAYS.
YOU MUST ORGANIZE YOURSELVES AROUND SEAN'S APARTMENT. YOUR POWERS ARE **NOT** MAGIC, **SEAN**. YOU ARE DEAD. YOU DON'T SHOW UP AT ALL. THIS WILL PROTECT YOU **ALL**.

WHAT ABOUT THE BAT?

MAKE IT THE SLIPCOVER WE SPOKE OF. QUELL ITS LIGHT. OTHERWISE, IT'S SAFE.

KEVIN, OF COURSE, MUST CEASE TO EXIST IN THE LEGAL SENSE. FROM **WITHIN** WHERE I AM GOING, I SHALL SYSTEMATICALLY DESTROY ALL EVIDENCE OF HIM. HE CAN NO LONGER TURN BACK. HIS WORLD HAS CRUMBLED.

SEAN, I LEAVE YOU A TASK, THE IMMENSITY OF WHICH YOU **CANNOT** CONCEIVE. I **BEG** YOU TO TELL ME THAT YOUR DOUBTS ARE DISPERSED, AND THAT YOU ACCEPT THIS SCENARIO.

I'VE DECIDED TO TAKE ON THIS CASE, AND YOU CAN BE **SURE** I WILL PURSUE ITS VERY RAPID CONCLUSION. I AM, AFTER ALL, A **DAMN** GOOD...

...EH...I...**WAS** A DAMN GOOD P.D.

AFTER ALL, I HAVEN'T REALLY A CHOICE.

HE NEEDS YOU. TRY NOT TO FIGHT WITH HIM.

YES.

LOOK OUT FOR HIM. HE'LL **LET** YOU.

YOU HAVEN'T LEFT US **MUCH** TO GO ON, DRAPES.

BUT HE **IS** CAPABLE, FAIR LADY.

FAREWELL, MAGICIAN.

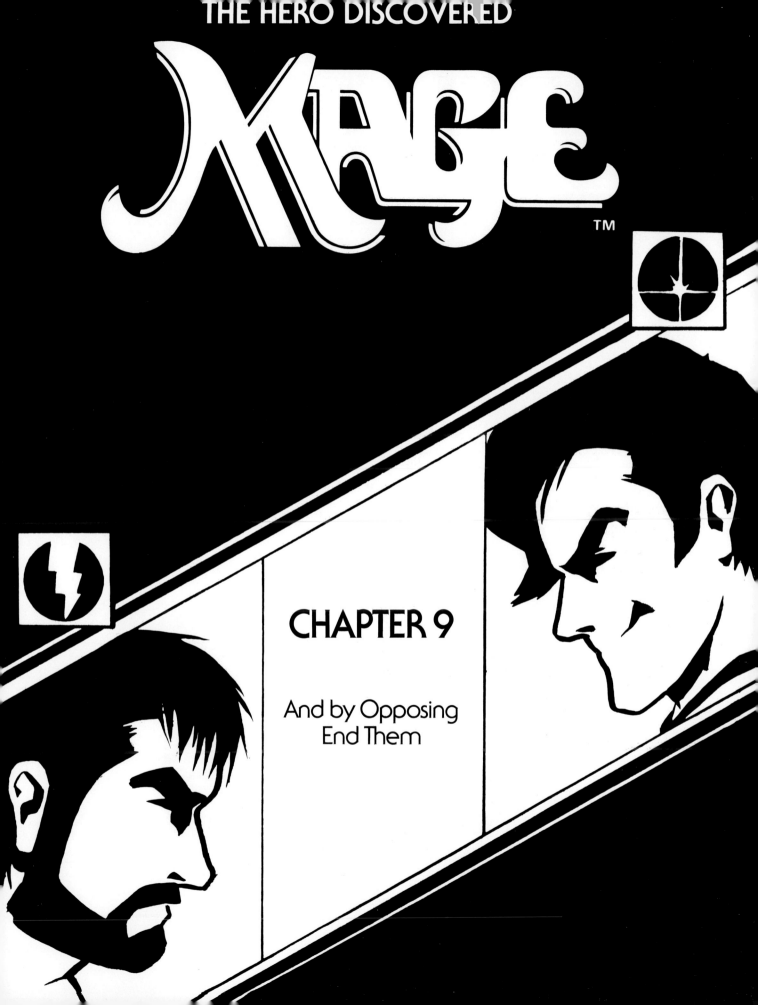

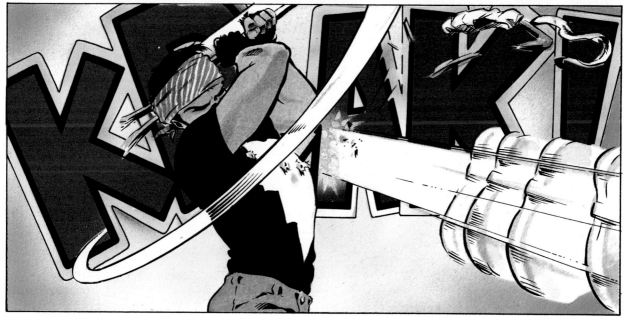

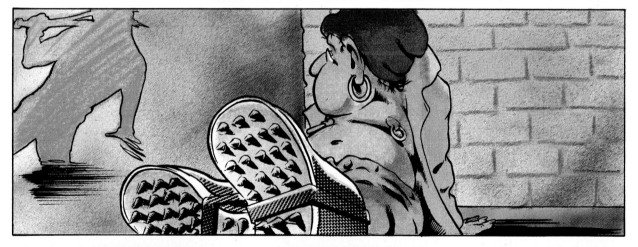

CHNK

LAZLO AND RADU JUST CALLED IN. THAT NEWEST LEAD THEY WERE CHECKING ON...

...TURNED OUT TO BE MATCHSTICK!

YES, I SURMISED. I FELT THE RED-CAP PHASE OUT.

THAT MAKES FOUR TIMES HE HAS FOOLED US.

AND IT'S ONLY BEEN FIVE MONTHS.

IT IS BECAUSE YOU HAVE NEVER KNOWN HIM. HE IS INCOMPLETE BUT FAR FROM INCOMPETENT.

I WOULD'VE THOUGHT HIM BLIND WITHOUT MIRTH.

SO YOU CAN SEE WHY IT IS SO IMPORTANT TO FIND HIM, WHY I MUST DEVOTE AS MUCH TIME AS POSSIBLE TO FINDING HIM.

EITHER HIM, OR WHERE HIS ACCURSED MAGE HAS GONE.

YOU STILL HAVE NOT FELT EVEN A GLIMMER?

SPORADICALLY, THERE IS A FLASH, BUT AS BRIEF AND FLEETING AS THE WEAKNESS IN A DRAGON'S EYE.

THINK HE'LL *EVER* CHANGE THAT SHIRT?

HERE.

APPARENTLY NOT AS LONG AS *MIRTH'S* LOCKED IN THAT COMPUTER.

WHAT'S THIS?

IT'S A LAUNDRY TICKET WE FOUND IN THE RED-CAP'S PANTS.

AT LEAST HE DOESN'T INSIST ON WEARING THE SAME ONE.

THANK GOD.

HI-DE-HO CLEANERS.

THINK *THAT'LL* EVER HAPPEN?

WHAT? MIRTH?

YEAH.

I COULDN'T TELL YOU, EDSEL. I REALLY KNOW NEXT TO *NOTHING* ABOUT THE MAN.

YOU'RE THE ONLY ONE OF US WHO SEEMS TO BE IN THIS THING OF YOUR OWN *FREE* WILL. YOU TELL ME.

BY THE WAY, I HAD TO WAYLAY THREE MORE RUNAWAY REPORTS ON YOU TODAY.

JUST *KEEP* SKRAGGING 'EM. I'LL GO BACK WHEN THIS IS ALL OVER.

AND *I* DON'T KNOW THAT MUCH ABOUT MIRTH, EITHER.

UH-HUH.

HI-DE-HO CLEANERS-- 477 N. 17TH.

WELL THEN...

...LET'S SEE IF I CAN *SCARE* UP A LITTLE INFORMATION.

YOU GONNA NEED HELP?

NO, I WOULDN'T THINK THIS WILL BE *THAT* TYPE OF OUTING.

STILL, I SUGGEST YOU STAY PUT HERE, IN CASE I WOULD NEED TO CONTACT YOU.

WHAT'S UP?

I'M GOING TO CHECK OUT THIS LAUNDRY TICKET. DON'T GO ANYWHERE.

MAYBE.

LOOK, IF ONLY TO *NOT* TIP OFF WHOEVER JUST MAY BE WATCHING OUT FRONT--*STAY PUT.*

I THINK THE BEGGAR ROUTINE HAS ABOUT *HAD* IT. WE'VE *GOT* TO ALTER OUR PLANS...

...AND THIS COULD TURN OUT TO *BE* SOMETHING.

...UM, WELL, Y'SEE, THAT'S FROM SOME OF THE STUFF WE LEASE TO THE GUYS OVER AT THE STYX.

THE STYX CASINO?

Y-YEAH, UH-HUH.

S-S-SEE, M-MY BOSS HAS PILED UP A LOT OF, *LIKE,* LEFTOVER CLOTHES OVER THE YEARS. HE LEASES SOME OF THEM OUT TO THE STYX. SPARE STUFF... Y'KNOW.

HMMM... WONDER WHY THE STYX WOULD DEAL WITH SUCH A LITTLE PLACE WAY ACROSS TOWN?

WHO USUALLY COMES IN TO PICK THIS STUFF UP?

I-IT'S USUALLY ONE OF THE PIT BROTH--*UH,* I MEAN, PIT MANAGERS.

WHAT DID YOU SAY?

*I-I-I STARTED TO SAY PIT BROTHERS...*C-CUZ THE FIVE PIT MANAGERS LOOK SO MUCH ALIKE. W-WE USED TO C-CALL THEM THE PIT BROTHERS BEHIND THEIR BACKS.

THESE ARE THE PIT MANAGERS OVER AT THE CASINO?

YES, SIR.

AND YOU SAY THEY ALL LOOK ALIKE?

KINDA.

KINDA?

W-W-WELL, ALMOST, *BUT* NOT QUITE. I-IT'S HARD TO EXPLAIN.

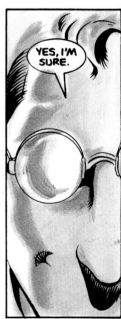

YES, I'M SURE.

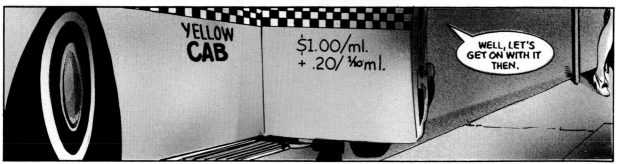

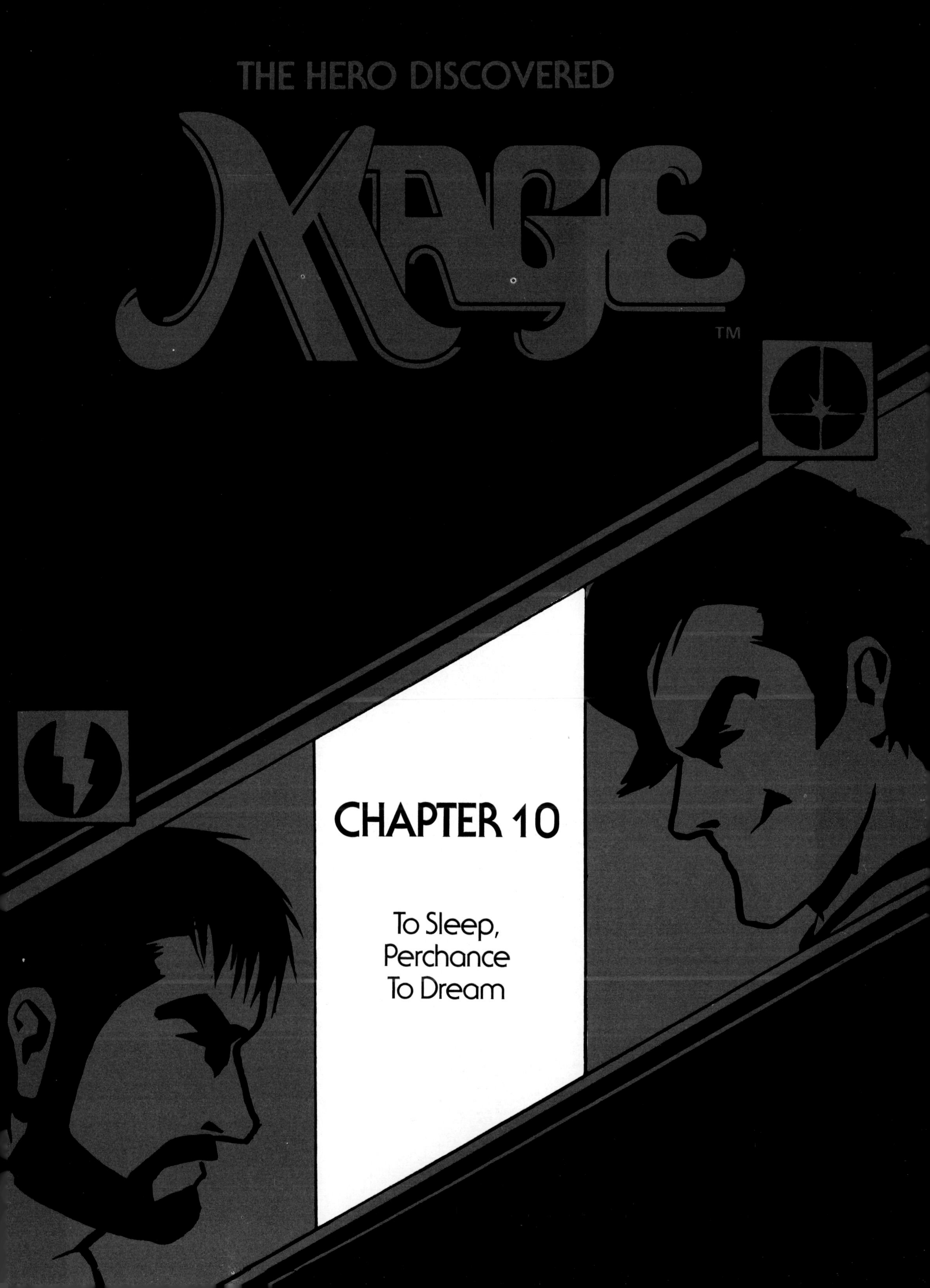

THE HERO DISCOVERED

# MAGE

™

# CHAPTER 10

To Sleep,
Perchance
To Dream

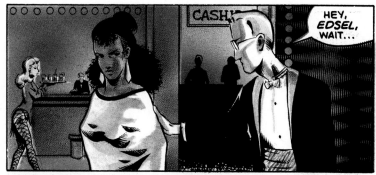

WELL, I GOTTA GO GET SOME THINGS READY FOR THIS PARTY. YOU'RE ON DECK, VINCE.

SURE THING, EMIL.

CHANGE A TWENTY.

CHECK.

DID HE SEE YOU?

NO, I DON'T THINK SO. WE WERE FAIRLY WELL HIDDEN.

WHAT DO YOU MEAN *HIDDEN*? WEREN'T YOU *INVISIBLE*?

RADU?

OH, YES, HE *SHOULDN'T* HAVE BEEN ABLE TO SEE US.

SHOULDN'T?

WELL, YOU SEE, EVERY COUPLE OF STEPS, HE KEPT STOPPING AND GLANCING OVER HIS SHOULDER-- ALMOST LIKE HE COULD *FEEL* WE WERE THERE.

WELL, WHAT DID YOU *LOOK* LIKE?

LIKE OURSELVES-- TRENCHCOAT, HAT. *PIET* WAS BUSY WHEN WE LEFT.

SO THAT MEANS WE'RE PROBABLY SAFE *NOW*. LAZLO...

...GO CHECK HIM OUT.

OKAY.

OOOOOPS--

OH-MI-GOD, EXCUSE ME, SIR! MUST'VE BEEN A HUNK OF LOOSE CARPET OR SOMETHING!

'S'OKAY.

WAITRESS! COME TAKE THIS MAN'S ORDER.

SNAP!

ONCE AGAIN, MY APOLOGIES, SIR.

HEY. NO PROBLEM.

WHAT CAN I GET YOU, SIR?

SCREWDRIVER. THANK YOU.

YOU KNOW, MAYBE HE DISCOVERED SOME WAY TO HIDE HIMSELF *COMPLETELY*-- FROM FATHER, FROM US...

AND *STILL* MOVE AROUND FREELY!

IF THAT'S SO, WE'RE IN *BIG* TROUBLE.

YOU SAID IT.

IT CAN'T BE *MIRTH*, YOU FOOLS. IF THERE'S ONE THING WE *CAN* BE SURE OF, IT'S THAT FATHER WILL FEEL THAT LITTLE SHIT AS SOON AS HE'S ANY-WHERE *NEAR* THIS PLANE. NO, SOMEHOW *YOU GUYS* SCREWED UP.

LOOK AT *MATCHSTICK* OVER THERE, EYE-BALLING OL' VINCE. MUST THINK *HE'S* THE REGULAR PIT BOSS. SOMEHOW, THEY SEEM TO KNOW *WHAT* THEY'RE LOOKIN' FOR--THEY JUST DON'T KNOW WHO.

I GUESS I'D BETTER INFORM FATHER. STAY HERE.

HERE?! YOU'RE SURE?

YES, OF COURSE I'M SURE.

I HAVEN'T SEEN THE GIRL YET, BUT THERE'S SOME OTHER FELLOW WITH HIM WHO SHOWED NO SIGNS AT ALL WHEN LAZLO TOUCHED HIM.

THE OTHERS THINK IT MIGHT BE MIRTH.

NO, THAT'S ABSURD. IF HE SHOWED NOTHING, THEN HIS LIFE FORCE IS NOTHING. POSSIBLY A GHOST.

ARE THEY UNITED, OR SPREAD OUT?

SPREAD OUT. MATCHSTICK'S PLAYING BLACKJACK AND STARING AT THE TEMPORARY PIT BOSS.

AMAZING. I MUST SEE ABOUT DEALING WITH THIS AT ONCE.

WE SHALL NEED SOMETHING TO LURE HIM, SOMETHING TO SUBDUE HIM AND SOMETHING TO BIND HIM.

THAT'S PRETTY DEMANDING.

COULDN'T WE TRY IT *OURSELVES*? YOU *DO* HAVE A DEDICATION SPEECH TO MAKE IN ABOUT HALF AN HOUR.

ARE YOU *KIDDING?!*

I CAN'T *DELAY* THINGS THAT LONG! THERE'LL BE OVER THREE HUNDRED PEOPLE WAITING FOR THAT SPEECH--

HE'S BECOMING LESS REFLEXIVE WITH THE POWER. HE COULD DISMEMBER YOU ALL.

SIMPLY DELAY THE OPENING SPEECH FOR AN HOUR OR SO. THAT WILL BE TIME ENOUGH FOR ME TO REST.

DO NOT QUESTION ME, EMIL! INVENT WHATEVER YOU MUST, BUT YOU *WILL* COVER MY DELAY!

THESE HUMANS ARE, AFTER ALL, AS CATTLE...

...LEADING THEM IS REALLY QUITE A *SIMPLE* TASK.

YOUR FORM HAS SHIFTED BACK.

I CAN RETRIEVE IT. ANOTHER SIMPLE TASK. ≥KOFF≤

AS IS THE LURING OF MATCHSTICK.

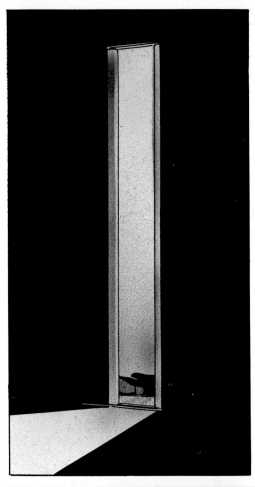

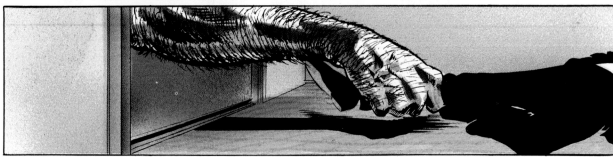

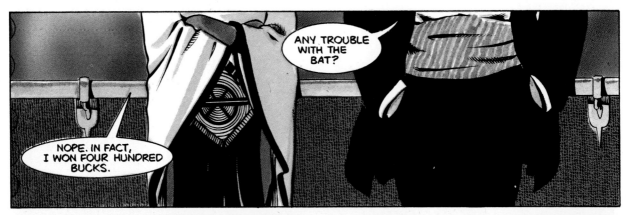

ANY TROUBLE WITH THE BAT?

NOPE. IN FACT, I WON FOUR HUNDRED BUCKS.

YOU'RE KIDDING.

NOPE.

SHIT.

WELL, I'M AFRAID MY EXPEDITION WASN'T QUITE AS FRUITFUL. THERE DIDN'T SEEM TO BE ANY CENTRAL PIT BOSS AT THE BACCARAT TABLES. THERE'S ONLY A HANDFUL OF TABLES AND EACH ONE'S CALLER SEEMED TO PRETTY MUCH RUN THINGS.

AND EVERYBODY AT THE TABLES SEEMED TO BE GOING TO THE PARTY...

...SO NO ONE WAS TALKING ABOUT IT.

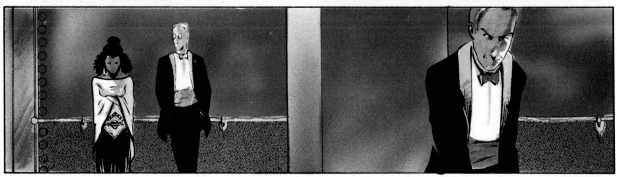

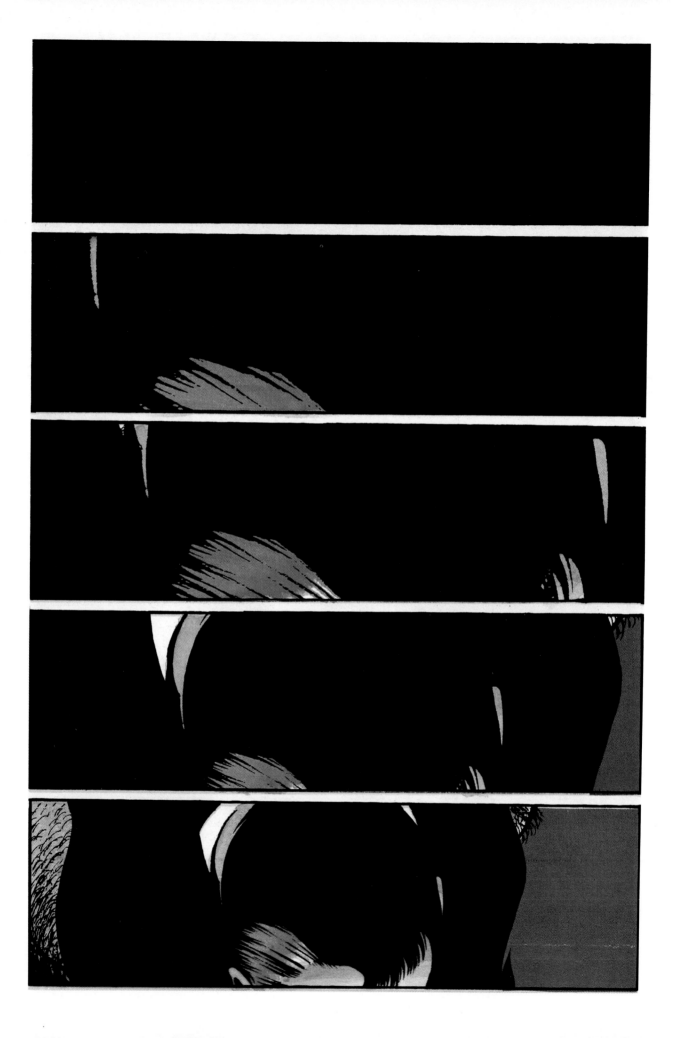

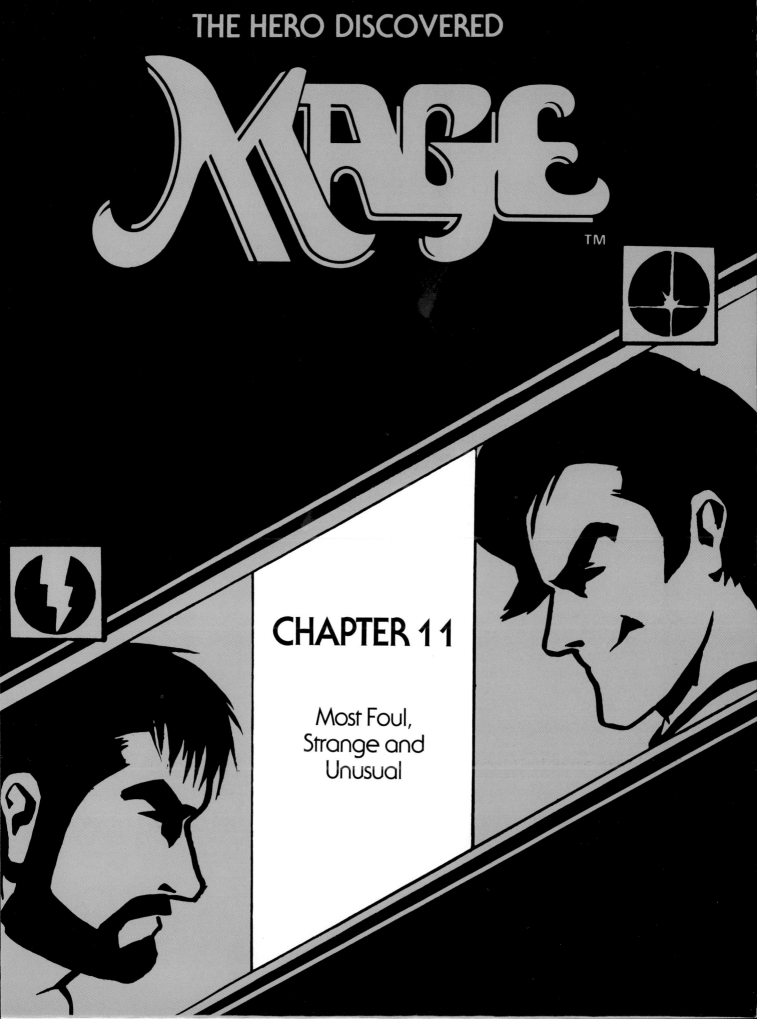

HE'S HALF AN HOUR LATE. NO GOOD.

GIVE HIM A LITTLE LONGER. HE *IS* SINGLE-MINDED SOMETIMES.

BUT, THIS ISN'T JUST *ANY* TIME. SOMETHING'S UP.

WHAT WAS THAT YOU SAID EARLIER ABOUT RED HAIR?

DAMN IT, THAT'S JUST IT. I *CAN'T* REMEMBER.

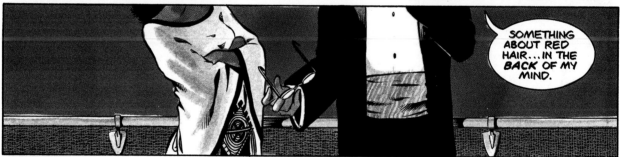

SOMETHING ABOUT RED HAIR... IN THE *BACK* OF MY MIND.

SHIT. MY MEMORY'S BEEN GETTING WORSE. STRAY THINGS... AND I CAN'T REMEMBER THEM.

C'MON, THINK.

WHO DID YOU SEE WITH RED HAIR TONIGHT?

WAIT! I'VE GOT IT!

COME NOW, MR. MATCHSTICK, SINCE MIRTH DISAPPEARED YOU HAVE HAD RUN-INS WITH MY "BOYS" FIVE TIMES. THE FIRST I ASSUME TO HAVE BEEN ACCIDENTAL--YET THEREAFTER YOU HAVE SUCCESSFULLY TRICKED THEM INTO ENCOUNTERING YOU.

I ALSO ASSUME YOUR NEW FRIEND, THE GHOST, TO BE MAINLY RESPONSIBLE FOR THESE CLEVER PLANS. SO, TELL ME, HOW IS IT HE IS SO VERY HELPFUL?

YES, I SEE.

NOW.

YAAHHH...

UNG---

OH GOD.

OH GOD.

YES, MR. MATCHSTICK?

P-P-PUBLIC DEF-FENDER...

A PLOTTER...

...WITH ACCESS TO INFORMATION.

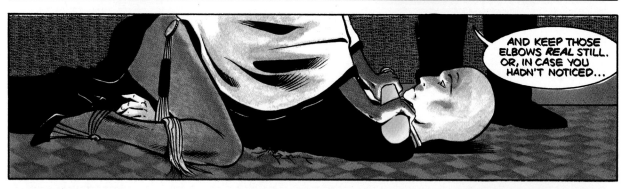

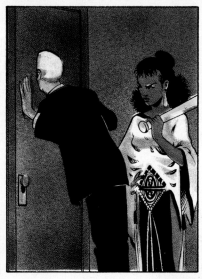

WHERE IS HE THEN, KEVIN?

YOU KNOW, I USED TO HAVE A CAT, ONCE. THOUGHT IT WENT WITH THIS PARTICULAR GUISE.

ANYWAY, ONE DAY IT BIT ME. I THREW IT DOWN THIS PIT.

COULD HEAR IT SCREECHING FOR ABOUT FOUR WEEKS BEFORE IT FINALLY QUIT-- OR HIT.

I SAY LET'S JUST DROP HIM AND BE DONE WITH IT.

SHUT UP, LAZLO.

OKAY, GET THIS. THIS OFFICE SEEMS TO SIT INSIDE SOME SORT OF HUGE PIT. BUT IT ALSO SEEMS TO SURROUND IT. THERE'S SOME SORT OF ENTRANCE ROOM TOO, APPARENTLY.

AND I'M BETTING IT'S RIGHT BEHIND THAT DOOR.

KEV?

YEAH, THEY'VE GOT HIM. THEY'RE TRYING TO SCARE HIM INTO TELLING THEM WHERE MIRTH IS.

GOT HIM HUNG OUT OVER THE PIT.

OVER THE PIT?!

EDSEL?

K.RAK

CHUKT

FATHER!

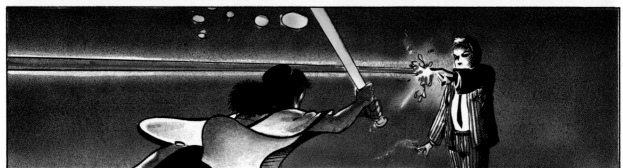

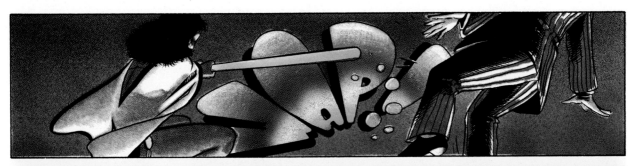

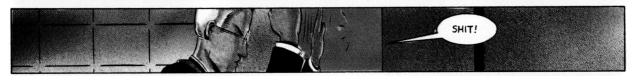
SHIT!

HEH...HEH...MY, MY, YOUNG LADY, YOUR BRAVERY GROWS WITH EVERY LIFE YOU LIVE, DOESN'T IT?

OH, THE TORMENTS I HAVE IN MIND FOR YOU WOULD MAKE AN OGRE'S SKIN CRAWL.

NO!

--HUH?

I SAID, NO!

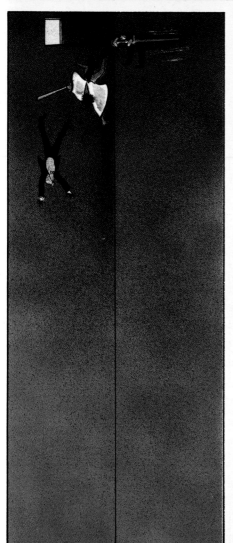

SEAN!

KEVIN! QUICK! THROUGH *THAT* DOOR AND THEN THE NEXT! PULL US THROUGH!

NICE JOB, EMIL.

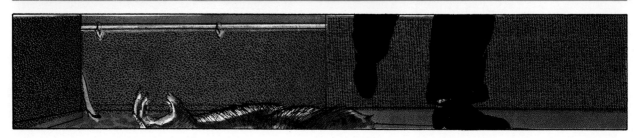

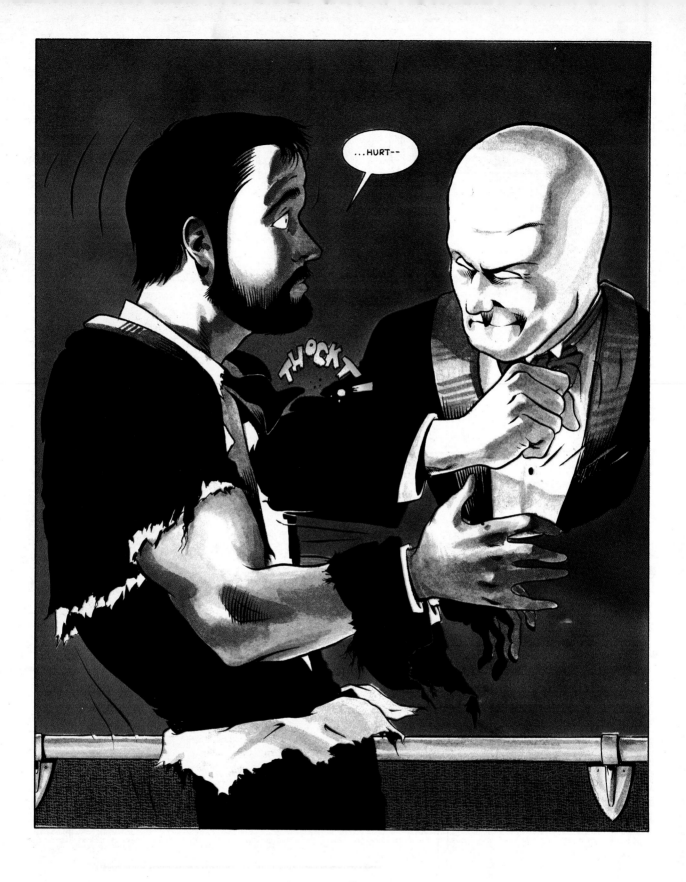

# THE HERO DISCOVERED

## continues from

## STARBLAZE GRAPHICS

Matt Wagner has written other graphic novels and comic titles including *Grendel,* published monthly by Comico, The Comic Company. His work is available at specialty shops and news-stands nationwide.

For further information, write:
Comico, The Comic Company
1547 DeKalb Street
Norristown, Pennsylvania 19401

The Starblaze Newsletter keeps you posted on upcoming titles and other interesting data.
(It's free, too!) Send your name and address to:
Starblaze Newsletter • The Donning Company/Publishers
5659 Virginia Beach Boulevard • Norfolk, Virginia 23502